Dear Parent:
Your child's love of reading starts here!

Every child learns to read in a different way and at his or her own speed. Some go back and forth between reading levels and read favorite books again and again. Others read through each level in order. You can help your young reader improve and become more confident by encouraging his or her own interests and abilities. From books your child reads with you to the first books he or she reads alone, there are I Can Read Books for every stage of reading:

SHARED READING
Basic language, word repetition, and whimsical illustrations, ideal for sharing with your emergent reader

BEGINNING READING
Short sentences, familiar words, and simple concepts for children eager to read on their own

READING WITH HELP
Engaging stories, longer sentences, and language play for developing readers

READING ALONE
Complex plots, challenging vocabulary, and high-interest topics for the independent reader

ADVANCED READING
Short paragraphs, chapters, and exciting themes for the perfect bridge to chapter books

I Can Read Books have introduced children to the joy of reading since 1957. Featuring award-winning authors and illustrators and a fabulous cast of beloved characters, I Can Read Books set the standard for beginning readers.

A lifetime of discovery begins with the magical words "I Can Read!"

Visit www.icanread.com for information
on enriching your child's reading experience.

For Abigail and Adam
—R.S.

I Can Read Book® is a trademark of HarperCollins Publishers.

Splat the Cat Gets a Job!
Copyright © 2018 by Rob Scotton
All rights reserved. Manufactured in China. No part of this book may be used or reproduced in any manner whatsoever without written permission except in the case of brief quotations embodied in critical articles and reviews. For information address HarperCollins Children's Books, a division of HarperCollins Publishers, 195 Broadway, New York, NY 10007.
www.icanread.com

Library of Congress Control Number: 2018938264
ISBN 978-0-06-269706-6 (trade bdg.)—ISBN 978-0-06-269705-9 (pbk.)

18 19 20 21 22   SCP   10 9 8 7 6 5 4 3 2 1   ❖   First Edition

Splat the Cat

Gets a Job!

Based on the bestselling books by Rob Scotton

Cover art by Rick Farley

Text by Laura Driscoll

Interior illustrations by Robert Eberz

HARPER

An Imprint of HarperCollinsPublishers

"Ta-da!" said Splat

as he came down the stairs.

He had on his newspaper-cat hat

and carried his newspaper-cat bag.

Splat was the new news cat!

It was Splat's first real job.

At bedtime, Splat was so excited

he could hardly sleep.

He couldn't wait to get started.

"Remember," Splat's mom said,

"you need to deliver all the papers

before school.

It's your job to get yourself

up and out of bed."

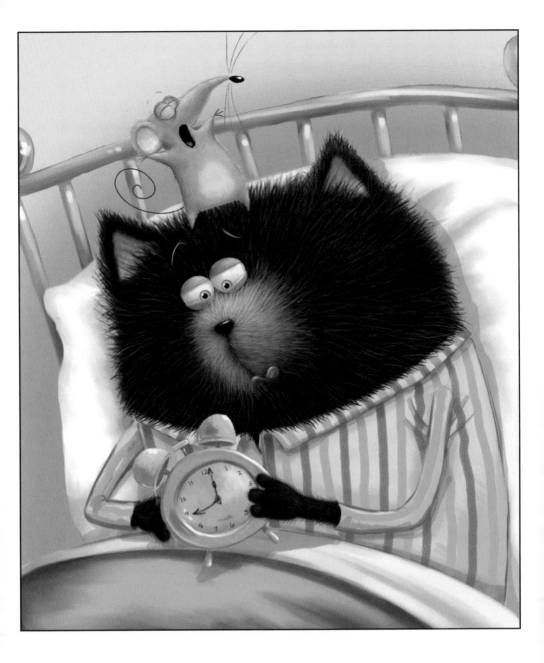

So Splat set his alarm clock

to go off extra early.

It went off at 6:00 a.m.

Splat hit the snooze button.

It went off again at 6:10.

Seymour hit the snooze button.

Splat snoozed until . . .

"Seven o'clock!" he cried.

Splat threw on clothes
and raced down the stairs.
He found the newspapers
on his front steps.
He stuffed them
into his news-cat bag.

Splat dragged the papers
from house to house.
It was a lot of work!

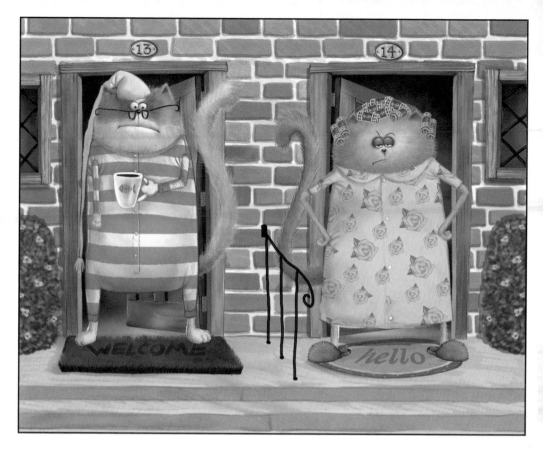

Finally, Splat came to the last two houses.

But his bag was empty.

He was short two papers.

"Sorry, Mr. Doodad,"

Splat said to his neighbor.

"Sorry, Mrs. Crankyankle."

To make matters worse,

Splat was late to school.

"Sorry, Mrs. Wimpydimple," he said.

"What happened to you?"

Kitten whispered.

At recess,

Splat told her about his new job.

"I'm a terrible news cat," he said.

"First I overslept.

Then I lost two papers."

"You just need a new alarm," Kitten said.

She loved to tinker.

After school,

Splat and Kitten got to work.

Splat dumped out his toy chest.

"Hmm," said Kitten.

Splat and Kitten made a plan.

They tested,

made some changes,

and tested again.

In the morning,

Splat's alarm went off.

He reached out to hit snooze.

The alarm hit back.

Splat was awake!

Splat packed up the newspapers.

Oof!

The bag was so heavy.

Splat was worried.

What if he lost papers again?

So Splat tried carrying them
a different way.
He rode from house to house,
tossing the papers.
A few landed just right.

Most of them did not.

"Sorry, Mr. Doodad," Splat said.

"Sorry, Mrs. Crankyankle."

Splat told Kitten his new problem.

"I'll never be able to toss papers

like the pros do," he moaned.

"You just need a slingshot,"

Kitten told Splat.

They made a plan.

Splat and Kitten tested,

made some changes,

and tested again.

The next morning,

Splat's alarm went off.

He reached for the snooze button—

but stopped just in time.

Splat packed up the papers,

rolling them just so.

Then Splat wobbled
from house to house.
Riding while aiming the slingshot
was tricky.

"Sorry, Mr. Doodad!" said Splat.

"Whoa!"

"Sorry again, Mr. Doodad,"

said Splat.

"Here's your paper."

29

"I can't do this!"

Splat told Kitten.

"You just need more hands," she said.

Splat looked at her.

"Kitten!" cried Splat.

"That's it!"

Splat made some changes to the plan.

"We could be a news-cat team!"

he said.

The next morning,

they did just that.